❧ MELA'S ❧
WATER POT

Based on a Folk Tale

WRITTEN BY SHELLY HURST LONNI
ILLUSTRATED BY HALA WITTWER

Long ago, a girl named Mela lived in a small village in India. Each day, it was her job to fetch water from the village well.

One day her mother handed her a very old water pot. "This pot was given to me by your grandmother," she said. "You may use it to fetch the water today. But take good care of it. It is very precious."

The village well was a busy place. Women were drawing water and visiting with their friends. As she waited in line, Mela glanced curiously at her pot. "Why would Mother give me this old pot?" she wondered. "We have nicer pots at home."

When Mela's turn came she filled her pot with the cool water and placed it carefully on her head.

6.

As she walked toward home, Mela did not notice the water trickling from a crack in the pot. She did not see the wet trail it left behind her.

The water splashed on the dry, cracked earth and touched a thirsty flower that was wilting in the sun. Slowly its drooping stem began to straighten.

As more water fell from the pot, the trail grew.
Little birds drank and bathed in its puddles.

The water flowed past a hot, dusty monkey.
He splashed some on his face to wash away the dust.
How clean and cool it felt.

As Mela walked on, her little river grew and brought good to all it touched. Flowers began to grow. Hot, thirsty cattle drank the water and were refreshed.

An elephant even put his trunk into Mela's pot for a cool drink, then sprayed the water into the air.

Finally Mela arrived home. When she took the old pot off her head, it was empty!

Then she noticed the small crack in the pot.

"Why did you give me a broken pot?" Mela asked her mother. "Now all the water has been wasted."

With a smile, Mela's mother turned her toward the path she had just walked. To Mela's surprise, she saw that the water from her pot had brought life, cleanliness, and joy to the plants, animals, and people in her village.

From then on, Mela loved to fetch water in the old pot, for she knew the secret of the water she carried.